NEWFOUNDLAND
AND LABRADOR

QUEBEC

PRINCE
EDWARD
ISLAND

NEW
BRUNSWICK

NOVA SCOTIA

FINISH

13

12

11

10

9

8

7

CARSON CROSSES CANADA

Linda Bailey

ILLUSTRATED BY
Kass Reich

TUNDRA BOOKS

Annie Magruder and her little dog, Carson, lived in the town of Tofino. Every day they walked beside the great Pacific Ocean. They loved the salt air, they loved their red house, and they loved their sweet life together.

Then one day Annie got a letter.

"Pack your suitcase," she told Carson. "My sister Elsie's sick, and she needs some cheering up!"

Carson didn't *have* a suitcase, but he got very excited when Squeaky Chicken went into the car. Annie packed camping gear and dog food. She filled a cooler with baloney sandwiches.

Then she and Carson piled into the car and drove east.

All morning, they drove in the rattlebang car. Carson scratched at the door. Were they there yet?

"Oh, no," said Annie. "It's a very long way. All the way across Canada. But there's a surprise when we get there. For you, Carson!"

Carson loved surprises. Squeaky Chicken had been a surprise.
Every time Carson chewed, he got a brand-new noise. *Skreeeee!*
Wheeeee! Iiiiiy!

On they drove, along twisty roads, through mountains as high as the sky.

"The Rockies!" said Annie. "If we were younger, we could climb them."

"RUFF!" said Carson.

"You're right," said Annie. "It *would* be rough."

That night, she put up their tent in the woods. Carson watched out for bears.

No bears came. But Carson was ready!

They rolled on down to a land of lumpy humps.
"Hoodoos," said Annie. "This is dinosaur country!"

When Carson saw the giant bones, he got very excited. Was *this* his surprise?

But before he could take a single bite, Annie dragged him away.

"Settle down, boy," she said.

Carson had never imagined a bone could get that big!

Next day, the land flattened out. Grain grew in carpets — yellow, blue, gold.

"Oh my," said Annie when they stopped for lunch. "Will you look at all that sky!"

But Carson was looking at the ground. There were grasshoppers everywhere! It took most of his lunchtime to catch one.

He ate it for dessert.

The next day was a "scorcher." That's what Annie said.
The sun beat hard on the highway.

Carson drooped all over. When he saw the lake, he was so
happy he tried to leap out the window.

Annie held him back. "Hang on, boy!" she said.

Soon they were both in Lake Winnipeg. Carson dog-paddled up to Annie and gave her a lick on the nose. For one cool, blue moment, they were *exactly* the same size.

After that, there were days of rocks and trees. Carson thought the trees would never end! He barked and barked out the window. Where was his surprise?

Annie gave him a pat. "It's still a long way to Elsie's."

That night they listened to the loons. *Ooo-wooooo. Ooo-hoo-hoo.*

"Oh my," said Annie. "Canada! Such a grand land to cross!"

And then came a grand sight indeed — a wall of water, thundering
down a cliff!

Carson yapped in amazement. He was used to water that stayed *flat*.

He and Annie watched till they were soaked all over. Then Annie went
to buy a souvenir of Niagara Falls.

Carson found a grassy spot and left a little souvenir of his own.

Next came a lively old city where people called Carson a *chien*.

"That's *dog* in French," whispered Annie.

They sat at a café and ordered a pie filled with pork. It was called *tourtière*.

Carson didn't care what it was called — as long as it had meat! He ate that pie in two bites.

And *still* they kept on driving. Carson was half asleep when Annie let out a yell. "Look! The Atlantic Ocean!"

Carson jumped up and ran — right to the water's edge. It smelled like the ocean back home. He sat with Annie and watched the tide go out. It left a sea of mud as far as the eye could see.

"Oh no!" cried Annie suddenly. "CARSON! DON'T YOU DARE!"

But Carson couldn't help himself. He rolled all over the seabed. Best mud ever!

The next day they crossed to an island of red and green. "Just like a postcard!" said Annie.

She stopped at a beach to buy lobster rolls. Carson ate his in one gulp.

"We're getting close," said Annie. "I hope you'll like your surprise."

But Carson knew what he'd *really* like . . .

Annie's lobster roll!

"We're almost there," said Annie as they left the island.

In the campground that night, there was fiddle music — so friendly and fast, it made everyone dance. Annie clapped and jigged. Carson chased his tail.

"Tomorrow," whispered Annie as they snuggled in their tent.

The rattlebang car drove onto a ferry . . .

And at last, they were FINALLY THERE!

A house stood waiting beside the ocean. It was red like the house back home. Out came a woman who looked like Annie. Her steps were slow, but her smile was as wide as the sea.

"Oh my dear," cried Elsie, and she hugged Annie hard. "I am some glad to see you!" The hugging went on for a very long time.

Carson let out a yip.

"Oh!" said Annie. "Do you want your surprise? Look! There he is."

Carson stared. His surprise was a dog! A dog who looked so much like Carson, it was like looking into a mirror.

"It's your brother," said Annie. "Digby! Do you remember?"

Carson barked with delight. This was even better than Squeaky Chicken! Carson hadn't seen his brother since they were pups. He couldn't believe how handsome Digby had grown!

As they unpacked the rattlebang car, Elsie smiled. She said seeing Annie and Carson was the best medicine in the world.

In the days that followed, they walked together beside the great Atlantic Ocean — Annie and Elsie, Carson and Digby. They loved the salt air. They loved the red house. And they loved their sweet time together.

It was grand!

For my sisters, Debbie and Wendy, and
sweet times together, past and future!
— LB

For Todd and his never-ending support
— KR

Text copyright © 2017 by Linda Bailey
Illustrations copyright © 2017 by Kass Reich

Tundra Books, a division of Random House of Canada Limited, a Penguin Random House Company

Library and Archives Canada Cataloguing in Publication
Bailey, Linda, 1948-, author
    Carson crosses Canada / Linda Bailey ; illustrated by Kass Reich.
Issued in print and electronic formats.
ISBN 978-1-101-91883-8 (hardback).—ISBN 978-1-101-91884-5 (epub)
    I. Reich, Kass, illustrator II. Title.
PS8553.A3644C37 2017   jC813'.54   C2016-905232-X
                                                  C2016-905233-8

Published simultaneously in the United States of America by Tundra Books of Northern New York,
a division of Random House of Canada Limited, a Penguin Random House Company

Library of Congress Control Number: 2016948511

Edited by Tara Walker and Jessica Burgess
Designed by Leah Springate
The artwork in this book was hand-painted in gouache with details added digitally.
The text was set in Bembo Book.

Printed and bound in China

www.penguinrandomhouse.ca

1 2 3 4 5   21 20 19 18 17

Penguin
Random
House
TUNDRA BOOKS

YUKON

BRITISH COLUMBIA

NORTHWEST TERRITORIES

NUNAVUT

ALBERTA

SASKATCHEWAN

MANITOBA

ON

START

PACIFIC
OCEAN

CARSON AND ANNIE'S ROUTE

1 Tofino

2 Cathedral Grove

3 Rocky Mountains

4 Dinosaur Provincial Park

5 Prairie farms

6 Lake Winnipeg

7 Great Lakes area

8 Niagara Falls

9 Quebec City

10 Bay of Fundy

11 Prince Edward Island

12 Cape Breton Island

13 Witless Bay